A Slip in Time

MAGGIE PEARSON

A Slip in Time

MAGGIE PEARSON

A & C Black • London

For Eleanor Isabel
(when she is old enough to read it)

This edition 2010
First published 2001 in hardback by
A & C Black Publishers Ltd
36 Soho Square, London, W1D 3QY

www.acblack.com

ISBN 978-1-4081-1505-3

A CIP catalogue for this book is available from the British Library.

Printed and bound in Great Britain
by CPI Cox and Wyman, Reading, RG1 8EX.

Contents

1

Fog!

There's nothing quite like a London pea-souper. Not any more. You don't get the right sort of smoke any more. If you wanted to mix up a real pea-souper, you'd have to travel back a good hundred years to begin with, to a cold winter's night with the river mist rolling up from the garbage dumps downstream. Mix equal parts of river mist and coal-fire smoke. Season to taste with the smell of horse dung, cabbage cooked to death and rubbish left festering in a hundred backalleys. Leave to settle till it's thick enough to scoop up by the shovelful and carry right through the house and out the back and never spill a drop.

That's your pea-souper.

Fog.

Fog wasn't so bad, if the place you called home was as near as you could get to the grating where the warm air curled upwards from the basement kitchen of Mrs Tidy's Hot Pie Emporium.

Fadge quite liked fog. Twining itself round him like a damp, oversized cat, licking at his grubby face.

Yes, fog was all right. Better than winter rain or sleet. Better than the wind that had been blowing the fine snow back, day after day, over the path he'd cleared so people could cross the road without getting their feet wet. You had to earn a penny or two where you could.

Later on, there'd be gentlemen rolling home from a night out on the town, losing their way in the old pea-souper and looking for an honest face to set them back on the straight and narrow. Good for a penny or two. Once one of them tossed him a golden guinea by mistake. But the Masher had taken it off him before Fadge got a chance to see if he could spend it without getting himself arrested.

The smell from Mrs Tidy's Hot Pie Emporium was singing a siren song to Fadge's nose. With expert fingers, he counted the coins in his pocket. Enough for a mutton pie to take away, but no sitting down in the warm.

Fadge sighed. He told himself it was early yet.

Not far away, a barrel organ started to play.

Fadge swept the slush off his crossing once more for luck, flicked a stray lick of fog off the end of his broom and settled down to wait.

2

The Great Detective

The sound of the television reverberated through the house, echoing in and out of every nook and cranny.

Grandad was hard of hearing. That was his excuse. Who did he think he was kidding? Jack wondered. Watching *Sherlock Holmes* videos back-to-back was just Grandad's way of pretending that Real Life wasn't happening.

'You'll like it when you get there, Dad,' Mum said for the zillionth time, as she whisked away the cup of undrunk tea from the table beside him and put another, fresher, one in its place. Jack could fill in the rest from memory, he'd heard it so many times. 'Much nicer than living in this big, draughty house all on your own. Sheltered housing! All your own bits and pieces. Someone within call if you need help.

And in the country, too!'

Silently, Grandad reached for the remote and turned up the sound.

Sherlock Holmes's voice boomed out: 'The vilest alleys of London, Watson, do not present a more dreadful record of sin than does the smiling and beautiful countryside.'

Mum flinched, rolled up her sleeves, and went to excavate another kitchen cupboard. She was finding stuff at the back of some of them – like half a tin of powdered egg with the lid rusted shut – that must be from the War.

Jack took refuge in the attic, the furthest away from both of them that he could get. 'Help yourself!' Grandad had told him. 'Take anything you want! Anything. Everything. Everything must go!' Like this was some kind of closing-down sale. Except no one was buying.

Gloomily, Jack gazed around the attic. There was stuff here older than Grandad. Older than Grandad's grandad, probably. Stuff so old it seemed to have taken root, weaving itself into the fabric of the building. Move the wrong thing and the whole house would come crashing down around your ears.

Utility furniture and rubbish pictures. China washbasins with matching jugs, odd rolls of wallpaper, Great-grandad's Home Guard outfit, the coat so stiff it stood up on its own with the helmet balancing on top, and half a bicycle. Stacks of dusty magazines tied up with string, and boxes and trunks in all shapes and sizes. He'd got to pick something, so as not to hurt Grandad's feelings. But what to choose? What to choose?

'Jack? Ja-a-ack!' Mum yelled from the kitchen, letting him off the hook.

He clattered gratefully back down the stairs. Mum pushed her purse into his hand. 'He's out of everything, almost. Milk, bread, All-Bran. I've made a list. Pop down the supermarket, will you, before they close.'

From the living room a woman's voice screamed, 'Danger, Mr Holmes? What kind of danger?'

'If we knew that,' Sherlock Holmes yelled back, 'then it would no longer be a danger.'

Grandad sourly mouthed every word in perfect lip-sync with them both.

Jack flung his Millwall scarf round his neck, stuffed Mum's purse in his pocket along with the shopping list and, still zipping up his jacket, fled down the front steps, into the gathering twilight.

'Don't forget the Case of the Blue Carbuncle!' Dr Watson roared after him.

The snow that had fallen half-heartedly over the last few days was melting to a slush, which gave off a faint mist as the temperature rose. It was like looking at the world through a fine net curtain. Unreal. Sounds were muffled by it. Footsteps. Voices. Traffic noise slowly fading into the distance.

Then came the cheerful sound of a barrel organ, ringing out clear and true. Some charity, collecting for the homeless, whatever. If he had some small change after the supermarket, he'd put it in the box on his way back. Mum wouldn't mind.

Jack turned and turned as he walked along, trying to get a fix on the music, which seemed to be near, then far, then all around.

So he didn't see it coming. Thick fog. Suddenly it was there, soft and yellow as a marmalade cat, rubbing itself up against him, twisting between his legs, then coiling upwards, reaching for his throat. The smell of it! Bad eggs and rotting fish, and something harsher, reaching deep down inside him. The streetlamps flickered and dimmed. Traffic sounds drifted far, far away. Then, just as suddenly as it had come, the fog suddenly slid down and lay curled about his ankles.

Jack looked around. Slowly, it dawned on him that he hadn't got a clue where he was. He didn't remember this street at all. Which was stupid; how far could he have wandered out of his way in the last couple of minutes? He strained his ears for the sound of traffic. All that came back was the clip-clop of horses' hooves.

And the barrel organ, grinding out the same tune.

What should he do? He knew what Grandad would say. 'You've got a tongue in your head, haven't you? If you don't know, ask!'

That's what he'd do. He'd ask the way, the first likely person he met. Simple. No problem.

3

Meeting in the Mist

Fadge weighed up the lone figure looming out of the fog and slush, moving silently towards him. Blue canvas trousers, like a sailor. Lace-up boots, white, like no boots Fadge had ever seen. Navy-blue padded coat, ditto. No buttons. A good, thick scarf, blue and white. He wouldn't mind a scarf like that. No hat.

That was a puzzler. A hat could tell you a lot about the person underneath. Which ones were good for a penny – or more – and which would only give you a thick ear. But no hat at all! Must be a foreigner. He was looking a bit lost.

'Cross the road, sir?'

'Sorry?' Jack stared at the scrawny, scruffy, smelly little kid, with the black concertina, that might have been a top hat in a previous life, balancing on top of his ears. He looked a bit small for a mugger. But he was brandishing an old garden broom in a very purposeful way.

Jack thrust his hands deeper into his pockets, keeping a tight hold of Mum's purse. He wasn't going to hand it over without a fight. Not to a snotty little kid half his size.

'Cross the road?' Fadge asked again, less hopefully. The customer was looking at him in a funny way. Like one of them might be soft in the head.

Jack looked up and down. There wasn't a car in sight. Not even the sound of a car. But maybe the kid had been told very firmly by his mum not to cross on his own.

'You want help to cross the road?' he said doubtfully.

'No,' said Fadge, puzzled. 'I thought p'raps you might.'

'No.'

They stood and stared at one another.

Foreign, decided Fadge. And soft in the head. Why would anyone think he – Fadge – needed helping across the road? He'd crossed that road more times than he'd had hot pies. A lot more. He looked the strange boy up and down. Good clothes. Maybe there'd be a reward for handing him back safe and sound, when his minders came looking.

Sometimes the only thing that kept Fadge going was the dream of one day getting a reward for handing in some piece of valuable lost property. A ring, a watch, a dog. He wasn't fussy. The idea that the lost property might come walking up to him on its own two legs had never occurred, but Fadge prided himself on being adaptable.

'Er,' said Jack. 'This is Garland Street, isn't it?'

'It is,' said Fadge. 'End to end, both sides and straight down the middle. Yes! Garland Street.'

Jack said, 'Everything looks different in the fog. But if this is Garland Street, the supermarket must be just along there, on this side. Right?'

Fadge shook his head. 'Wrong. No market down there.'

'I don't want a market. I want a shop.'

'You said the market.'

'I said the supermarket.'

'You've got me there.' Fadge had a bit of a scratch while he paused for thought. Stick with him, he decided. If he was so keen to see a shop...

'There's only one shop down here,' said Fadge. 'Come on. I'll show you.'

And though the smell of Mrs Tidy's Hot Pie Emporium was calling him in quite the opposite direction, Fadge set off, broom in hand, with Jack trailing behind.

The blinds had been pulled down over the shop windows by the time they got there, shutting out the dull, dank evening. But there was still enough light showing round the edges for Jack to read the lettering painted on the glass.

'Jas Rowbotham and Sons. Ironmongery. Hardware. Household Sundries. I've never seen this place before.'

'How do you know what it is,' demanded Fadge, 'if you've never seen it before?'

'It's written up, stupid. Can't you read?'

'No.'

'Not even a bit? You must go to school.'

'I've got no time for school,' Fadge said stoutly. 'I've got to work. If I don't work, I don't eat.'

'Oh.'

'I've got my own broom!' added Fadge, brandishing it.

'Er, yes,' Jack agreed. He squinted up at the flickering streetlamps. 'Are those gaslights? I don't remember gaslights.'

'They're new,' said Fadge.

'And where are all the cars? There are always cars parked, all along here. Are those cobblestones? They are, aren't they? I don't believe this.' He was beginning to get the uncomfortable feeling that he'd wandered into one of Grandad's *Sherlock Holmes* videos. No! Daft idea. Try something else. 'Are you a ghost?'

'No. Are you?'

'Course not. Look; I've got to go.'

'No!' Fadge saw his hopes of The Reward getting ready to fade back into his dreams. Then came inspiration, flashing like a November rocket through the murky sky: 'Let's go somewhere we can talk. You got money?'

'Er, yes.'

'I know just the place. Come on!'

4

The Pie Shop

Mr Tidy, his face round and glistening as one of his wife's home-made pies, looked up and saw a familiar, battered top hat hovering level with the pie-shop counter.

'What's it to be, young Fadge?'

'Two mutton pies, with all the trimmings, and two pints of best,' ordered Fadge.

'Business doing well, then?' enquired Mr Tidy, setting the two plates down on the counter top and reaching for two pint tankards.

'He's paying.' Fadge jerked a thumb towards the boy beside him, who was staring round the room as if he'd never seen the like in all his born days.

A rum sort of boy, thought Mr Tidy. No older'n Fadge, but tall as me. Rum sort of coat. Bit like an eiderdown.

'How much?' asked Jack, fumbling for Mum's purse. Mum wouldn't mind. She was always on about the poor and hungry. 'There's a pound. Is that enough?'

A very clean boy, thought Mr Tidy, taking the coin without looking at it. Unnaturally clean. He tossed it into the till.

The coin chinked once and Mrs Tidy, from a standing start at the far corner of the room, was on to it before it had a chance to settle.

Bets had been placed, won and lost, on Mrs Tidy's fine tuning where money was concerned. 'Foreign!' she announced, holding up Jack's pound, slapping it back down on the counter, triumphant. 'We don't take foreign.'

It was on the tip of Jack's tongue to argue that this was English money, with the Queen's head on and everything, but he had a feeling it wouldn't get him anywhere.

Fadge sighed and felt in his pocket for his day's takings, spreading the coins out on the counter.

'Sorry,' said Jack, taking his pound back again. 'Don't worry about me. I wasn't hungry anyway.' Not once he'd seen the inside of the pies people were eating, more fat than meat. The drink looked suspiciously like the beer Grandad had given him to taste once. 'Nobody likes it the first time,' said Grandad. 'You have to work at it.'

'You go ahead,' said Jack.

As soon as Mrs Tidy's back was turned, 'Drink's on the house,' whispered Mr Tidy, tipping Fadge the wink. 'I can't pour it back in the barrel, can I? You can owe me for the trimmings.' He pushed one small, brown coin back across the counter.

Fadge slipped it in his pocket and fixed his mind firmly on The Reward.

They found themselves a free table, between two tall wooden settles, and sat down, facing one another.

'What did he call you?' asked Jack. 'Fadge?'

'That's right.' Fadge tucked in, making the best of things. Since he'd had to buy the meal after all, he might as well enjoy it. 'What's yours?'

'My name? Jack. Jack Farthing.'

Fadge put down his knife and fork and stared open-mouthed. 'Well, there's a turn-up and no mistake! That's my name!'

'I thought you just said it was Fadge?'

'Yes.' Fadge rummaged in his pocket and pulled out the small, brown coin again. 'That's a fadge. A farthing. Jack Farthing – Fadge!'

It was, as he said, a turn-up, thought Jack. What were the chances of bumping into someone with the same name as you? But then, what were the chances of any of this being real anyway? He was dreaming, that was it. But the film of grease that did duty for a tablecloth felt like real grease under his fingers. The fug of kitchen steam mixed with tobacco smoke, thicker than the fog had been, was real enough to set up a tickling in his throat.

A voice said, 'Here! Take a swig of that!'

Jack picked up the tankard that was pushed in front of him and sipped at it. Beer! Ugh! But it stopped the cough.

The two of them seemed to have turned into four. There was a big lad sitting beside Fadge, boxing him in beside the wall. He wore a red velvet jacket worn down to white cotton at the wrists and elbows, a silk scarf dashingly arranged to cover the worst of the soup stains on his shirt front, and a brown bowler hat that was far too good for him.

'Well, well!' said the big lad, looking round the smoky room. 'This is nice! And how's life treating you, young Fadge?'

'Mustn't grumble, Masher,' muttered Fadge, grimly shovelling in forkfuls of mutton pie till his cheeks were bulging like a hamster.

'Mustn't get too fat, neither,' muttered the Masher, sliding Fadge's plate across to himself. 'Or you'll be no use to me at all.' He snapped his fingers. Dumbly, Fadge handed over his knife and fork and watched as the rest of his dinner began to disappear down the Masher's throat.

The Masher swallowed, burped and nodded to the scarecrow figure perched on the settle beside Jack. 'Rusty!'

A claw-like hand reached out and pushed the pint pot that had once – in Fadge's dreams – been his, away from Jack and back across the table for the Masher to take a good, long swig.

Jack sneaked a glance at the well-named Rusty. Rust-red hair straggling out from under a filthy cap, rusty-black coat, rusty-brown dirt under his fingernails and a voice, when he spoke, which wasn't often, that sounded like

24

coffin nails rubbing together for company.

Jack, easing himself away, in case any of the rustiness should rub off, felt the Masher's good eye fixed on him. 'Who's this, then?' demanded the Masher.

'That's Jack,' said Fadge.

'Jack who? Jack Frost? Jack Sprat? Jack Tar? Ha ha! Jack-in-the-box?'

'Jack Farthing,' said Jack, doing his best not to flinch away from the Masher's dragon-breath. Stand up to bullies, Grandad always said. Don't try to pick a fight, just look 'em in the eye and show 'em you're not afraid.

The Masher raised one eyebrow (a trick he'd spent hours practising in front of the mirror). 'Family o' yours, Fadge? You actually got family?'

'Yes,' said Jack.

'That's all right, then,' said the Masher. 'We can talk. I got a job for you, young Fadge. I need a snakesman. Tonight.'

Fadge wriggled uncomfortably. 'I don't know about tonight, Masher. Tomorrow, maybe.'

'Tonight.'

'I don't know.' Go off with the Masher

25

and leave his prize goose sitting here before it had had a chance to lay its golden egg? On the other hand, the Masher wasn't in the habit of taking 'no' for an answer. 'You said yourself, Masher, I'm getting over-large for a snakesman.'

'You'll do for this. I measured the jump already.'

'I gotta look after Jack.'

'I'll come with you,' said Jack. He didn't know what a snakesman was, or where Fadge was supposed to jump. What he did know was that sticking with Fadge had to be better than being left on his own in a strange town. A strange time, even.

Fadge beamed at him, gratefully.

The Masher nodded. 'You can come if you want. I can use a fourth man. Specially one that ain't known.'

Fadge said, 'All right, then, Masher. You talked me into it.'

5

Snakesman at Work

Outside, the fog seemed to have cleared completely. It happened like that sometimes. But look into any dark corner, up any alleyway and you'd see it curled there, lurking, biding its time, ready to pounce.

It would have to move fast to catch the Masher, striding out on his long legs, while the rest of them jogged along behind. Down the street they went and round a corner. Across the next street, and down an alleyway, diving into a sudden bank of thick fog and surfacing again opposite a row of neat little terraced houses.

'That's the one,' the Masher pointed, stopping as suddenly as he'd set off. 'That's the doctor's house. Third from the far end. You got that? I'm talking to you, Jack Farthing!'

'Oh! Right!' said Jack. 'But why are you telling me? I don't need a doctor.'

'Yes, you do. There's a poor old lady, sick and like to die, if you don't fetch the doctor to her, quick sharp.'

Jack was opening his mouth to say 'What old lady?' and 'Why me?' when the Masher gave him a shove. 'Off you go, then. What are you waiting for?'

'You haven't told me where she lives,' said Jack.

'Where she lives?' The Masher looked blank. He turned to Fadge, as if to say, 'Do I have to do his thinking for him?'

Fadge shrugged.

'The Spread Eagle,' rasped Rusty.

'That's a pub, right?' said Jack.

'No!' exclaimed the Masher, spreading his arms wide and flapping them up and down. 'It's a great, big, live bird! 'Course it's a pub, you cloth-head!'

'Is that where she is?' offered Fadge. 'The Spread Eagle?'

The Masher beamed. 'Got it in one, young Fadge!'

'Took bad, she was,' said Fadge, 'right

outside the door, an' the landlord, like a Christian gentleman, he took her in. Right, Masher?'

The Masher nodded.

'Go back down the alley, Jack,' said Fadge. 'Turn left at the end, instead of right, back the way we came. Then first right and second left and keep straight on. The Spread Eagle. You can't miss it. Ask for Mrs – Mrs –'

'Smith,' grated Rusty, like he was already sliding the old lady's first coffin nail into place.

'Granny Smith,' nodded the Masher.

'Just leg it, the first chance you get,' Fadge muttered out of the corner of his mouth. 'I'll meet you,' he glanced from Rusty to the Masher, 'the same place we met before.'

The Masher, with his hand clamped fast to Fadge's shoulder, was already hurrying him away, with Rusty close behind.

'Where are you going?' demanded Jack.

'We got to fetch the old woman's family, before she snuffs it. Eh, Fadge? Eh, Rusty?'

'The priest,' wheezed Rusty. 'She's asking for a priest.'

Jack caught Fadge's desperate look, as he was dragged away. Fadge was well worried, but it wasn't about some poor old lady.

Then the Masher whisked them round a corner and the only evidence they'd ever been there was the fading sound of Rusty coughing. Jack was on his own after all, still with a load of shopping to get and not the foggiest idea how to find his way back to Grandad's. There was nothing he could do about it, not just at present. Not that he could see.

So he set off down the narrow street of terraced houses until he came to the third one from the end, where a plump young man in shirtsleeves was busy polishing a brass plate on the wall beside the front door.

'Excuse me,' said Jack.

The young man gave a guilty start and spun round, trying to hide his polishing cloths behind his back.

'I'm looking for the doctor,' said Jack.

'You've found him! John H. Watson, M.D.' The young man stuck out a hand to shake, noticed the cloth still in it, and hid it behind his back again. 'My housekeeper!' he explained. 'Old lady. Bad chest.' He thumped himself twice on the chest to demonstrate. 'Outside work. Not good for her in this pea-souper.'

He seemed very young for a doctor, with a round baby face, bright, innocent eyes and a shock of curly hair. The moustache looked like a cheap disguise. But the brass plate said Dr J.H. Watson, M.D. So Jack gave him the message about poor old Granny Smith, sick and like to die, and the others going off to fetch her sorrowing family etcetera, and before he was halfway through, the young man was shrugging on his coat and racing upstairs for his doctor's bag (very shiny, very new), then down again, exclaiming, 'Oh, this is exciting! My first call-out! My first emergency! Where's my hat? My hat! My hat! I can't go without my hat!'

'Can't you?' said Jack.

'Of course not! Must look the part! Doctor must wear a hat. Imagine it, if a doctor came to call, looking like a … a butcher, say! Would you believe he could make you better?'

'I suppose not.'

'Of course not! Ah, here it is! Hanging on the hook behind the door. Off we go, then!'

Off they went. Down the road and through the alley, turn left at the end.

A thought struck Jack. 'Dr Watson,' he

said. 'You're not *the* Dr Watson, are you? The friend of Sherlock Holmes?'

'Shylock – ?'

'Sherlock.'

'Sherlock … Holmes, did you say? Odd sort of name.' He shook his head. 'No. Doesn't ring a bell.'

Of course it didn't. There was no such person. Never had been. Though Grandad said people from all over the world still wrote to the Great Detective at 221B Baker Street, asking him to solve their problems.

Did Fadge say second right, then first left? Or the other way round? Second right, Jack decided. Poor Fadge. Jack couldn't forget the worried look on his pinched face before the Masher whisked him out of sight.

Nothing worried Dr Watson. With John H. Watson, M.D. on hand, you just knew everything was bound to turn out all right. Jack couldn't help wishing that he'd met Dr Watson before he met Fadge.

Turn left. Soon be there. He was worried about Fadge. Leaving him with the Masher. And Rusty. There was something going on. Some reason they wanted him out of the way.

'Dr Watson,' said Jack. 'Do you know what a snakesman is?'

6

A Human Tug of War

In the dim alleyway that ran along the back of the terrace, Fadge stood beside the Masher, looking nervously up at a small, rectangular window. 'It's smaller than the last one, Masher.'

'We been through this before. Get your head and one shoulder through and the rest'll follow, easy as slicing butter.'

'It's awful high. What if I make a noise coming down the other side?'

'The house is empty. Jack Farthing's seen to that.'

All the same, there was something not quite right. Fadge could feel it in his bones. He peered towards the end of the alley, where they'd left Rusty on guard. 'Where's Rusty gone?'

'He's still there.'

'I can't see him.'

'Course you can't. Rusty's the best in the business.' That was true. The way Rusty lurked, passers-by rarely took him for anything more than their own shadows. The Masher gave a low whistle and a sound came back like rats suddenly disturbed, then settling again. That was Rusty. Rusty could do rats, cats, dogs, horses and half a dozen birds more lifelike than the real thing. It was just the human voice he could never quite get right.

'Up you go!' said the Masher. 'We haven't got all night.'

Fadge found himself lifted up and swivelled halfway through the narrow window before he knew it. He stretched out his arms into the dark and found the top of a cupboard or a table. A quick wriggle and a handspring down to the floor. And he was in. Standing in somebody's larder by the look of it in the pale moonlight.

Fadge made straight for the door, and found it locked.

He went back to the window. 'Door's locked, Masher. We're out of luck. Can you help me out?'

'You stay there!'

'What?'

'Stay there and do as I say. Look around you. Can you see a chicken?'

'A chicken, Masher?' Not content with stealing Fadge's dinner, the Masher was going to all this trouble to steal someone else's? 'What sort of a chicken?'

'Plucked. All ready for cooking. Look around you, Fadge!'

'I'm looking, Masher! Get out of the light. I'm looking.'

'It's there, Fadge! It's got to be!' The Masher, on tiptoe, pressed his face up close to the open window.

Of course the chicken was there. Fadge had seen it the moment he dropped to the floor. There wasn't much else. A few jars. A few vegetables. Half a loaf of bread. Fadge looked round in vain for a knife to cut it with and something to spread on it. Jam. Butter. A bit of beef dripping would be favourite. Nothing. He tried the door again.

'Fadge? What you doing, Fadge?'

'Nothing.'

'You found it?'

'What if I have? What's it worth?'

'Just give it to me. Pass it to me out of the window.'

'No.'

'All right. Sixpence?'

'I reckon it's worth more than that,' Fadge said thoughtfully.

'How much more?'

'Make me an offer.'

Then suddenly, 'Masher!' Rusty rasped in the Masher's ear.

The Masher, taken by surprise, somehow managed to crack his head on the top of the window frame and his chin on the sill, both at the same time.

'I gave the signal, Masher, but you never heard me! They've come back!'

Behind him, Fadge could hear footsteps coming through the house, and voices.

'Help me out!' pleaded Fadge.

'Give me that chicken.'

'What about me?'

'Give us the chicken, then we'll help you out.'

'You won't.'

'We will!'

The feet and the voices were just the other side of the door. The key was turning in the lock.

'It's both of us, or nothing!' Fadge stuffed the chicken up his shirt and leapt for the window.

Two pairs of hands grasped his wrists. But another four hands now had hold of his ankles.

There was a very short tug of war. Fadge and the chicken together were never going to fit through that window.

Fadge heard Jack's voice. 'It's all right, Fadge! I've told him! I told him they made you do it!'

But the Masher and Rusty still held him fast. Fadge kicked and wriggled and yelled fit to wake the dead three streets away.

As the first window slammed open and a head poked out to ask who was being horribly murdered on their doorstep, the Masher and Rusty let go and ran for it.

Fadge shot back into the larder like a human cannonball, and landed on something soft. The chicken soared into the air, hovered for a moment near the ceiling, then plummetted down to perch on his chest. 'Oooff!' Fadge lay for a moment, letting his arms and legs shrink back to their proper size.

'Gerroff!' growled Jack, from underneath him.

'Well, well!' said Dr Watson. 'Isn't this exciting!'

7

Chicken Surprise

Roughly ten minutes later the three of them stood round the kitchen table, staring hard at the chicken from three different sides. It didn't look too bad, considering what it had been through. There was stuffing dribbling from one end, and the left wing stuck out at an odd angle, as if the chicken was resting on its elbow, waiting for them to make up their minds.

'This friend of yours – is he specially fond of chicken?' asked Dr Watson, frowning.

Fadge shook his head.

'Anyway,' said Jack, 'he couldn't have been hungry. He'd just eaten Fadge's dinner.' He had the creepy feeling the chicken was looking at him, sizing him up. He edged out of its line of sight (not that it could see anything, having no head) and the others followed him, processing round the table.

The doctor twirled one end of his moustache, giving it a lop-sided look, as if it was starting to come unstuck. 'Could it have been a joke, do you think? Say he was put up to it by someone I know. Medical students. Yes? No.' He shook his head. 'I would have been sorry to lose it. Chickens don't come cheap.'

Jack toyed with the idea of making some crack about chickens not coming cheap, only chicks going 'cheep'. But thought better of it.

'My housekeeper –' the doctor began. 'Hrrm!' He cleared his throat. 'I'll come clean. I have no housekeeper. Can't afford it. Mrs Hudson's very good, though. She comes in twice a week. The rest I manage for myself, but it doesn't do to let people know.'

'Bad for the image?' suggested Jack. 'Like going out without your hat?'

'Exactly! Which is why you caught me polishing my brass plate under cover of darkness. I can't afford to eat chicken, either, as a rule. But this is a special occasion. A friend of mine – another doctor – is passing through tomorrow, on his way to take up a practice down in Southsea. Bit of a celebration, yes? I asked Mrs Hudson to buy me a chicken and leave it ready to pop in the oven.' He gave the chicken a doubtful look. 'I suppose it'll still be all right, once it's cooked.'

'I think p'raps you ought to wash it,' said Jack.

The doctor looked even more doubtful. 'What about the stuffing? Excellent stuffing Mrs Hudson makes! Don't want it waterlogged.'

'You could scoop it out,' suggested Fadge. 'Stuff it back in after.'

'Good thinking!'

The doctor rooted round until he found a spoon and a basin. He started scraping out the chicken while Fadge held it. Jack took charge of the basin, tipping it underneath the gaping neck, so not a scrap of Mrs Hudson's excellent stuffing would be lost.

At the third scoop, there was a 'chink' of spoon on metal.

'What's this?' said Dr Watson. He bent down and peered inside.

'This' seemed to be something solid mixed in with the squidgy stuffing. A glint of gold. A

42

gold chain! A gold chain leading back inside the bird. Gently the doctor drew it out and gently... gently...

Fadge and Jack watched open-mouthed. It was as if that chicken was laying a golden egg. Egg-shaped it was, but flatter, and studded with red and green stones. A golden pendant on a golden chain.

'That's what they were after!' breathed Jack. 'Not the chicken at all.'

'They ought to have told me,' muttered Fadge.

The doctor washed the pendant clean, holding it over the sink in his left hand, while he worked the pump briskly with his right.

'But how did they know?' demanded Jack. 'How did it get in there?'

Fadge said, 'Can I hold it? Please?'

He took it reverently, but firmly, so as not to drop it. As if he was afraid it might break. 'Gold!' he thought. Gold and jewels beyond his wildest dreams. He rubbed his fingers over the pendant, feeling the shape of it, the warmth of it. No more sleeping in the cold. No more being hungry. Then he felt a tiny 'click' and the pendant sprang open. It wasn't a pendant; it was a locket.

Inside was what might have been a portrait, if you looked at it from far enough off (like halfway down the street in a bad light). Close to, it was nothing but a collection of smudges, pink and black and purple streaked with gold.

'Well, well!' said the doctor. 'What are we to make of that? May I?' He took back the locket, and started examining it from every angle, holding it up to the light.

'P'raps some kid did it for his mum,' suggested Jack, remembering all his pictures from playschool that Mum still kept. Cringe-making stuff.

'Perhaps,' nodded the doctor. He peered a bit more, then, 'Hm!' he said thoughtfully. He snapped the locket shut and slipped it in his waistcoat pocket.

'Hey!' protested Fadge, indignantly, but faintly.

'What do we do now?' asked Jack.

'Why,' said the doctor, 'we must set about finding the owner.'

'What about finders keepers?' demanded Fadge.

'Shut up, Fadge,' said Jack, not unkindly.

'You can't just keep a thing if there's any chance of finding the owner.'

'How are we going to do that, then?' Fadge bit back scornfully.

'I think,' said Dr Watson, 'a visit to the butcher's shop is called for.'

So off they went, after a short delay while they all hunted for the doctor's hat again. Then there was a quick detour down the back alley, so Fadge could collect his broom.

Now and again, as they went along, Fadge thought he saw a movement in the shadows, a thickening of the darkness that might be Rusty. On the other hand, if he thought it might be, then it probably wasn't. Which didn't make him feel any better.

8

The Butcher's Tale

The butcher's shop was tiny, with sawdust strewn on the tiled floor for mopping up the blood, and festooned down either side with dead meat; like stepping into Bluebeard's wardrobe. At the far end stood a thick, pine table scored over and over by the wicked-looking cleaver in the butcher's hand. Jack and Fadge were quite happy to wait outside the open shop front, while the doctor went in and asked about the chicken sold to Mrs Hudson that afternoon.

Nothing wrong with his chickens! declared the butcher. (*Thunk!* agreed the cleaver, slicing off a lamb chop and sinking itself in the table underneath.) Show him the customer who'd ever had a word to say against them! Mrs Hudson? (The cleaver pulled itself free.

Dr Watson took a step back.) Been shopping with him these eight years – the cleaver drew a figure of eight in the air – had Mrs H, and never a word of complaint. So what if said chicken had spent a moment or two on the ground during the excitement? Hadn't he dusted it off most carefully? And knocked sixpence off the asking price? (The cleaver was fairly dancing now, conducting an invisible orchestra.)

What excitement? Ah! Pity they hadn't been there to see it. Late afternoon, it was. Suddenly, at the top of the street – the cleaver became one arm of a signpost – a woman screams, 'Stop! Thief!' This big lad dressed in red comes running down the street – knocks over the outside table (*swish!* went the cleaver) – together with the chicken that had Mrs Hudson's name on it. And the big lad – most polite, most thoughtful – picks the chicken up and dusts it down and puts it into the butcher's own hands before running on (*swash!* went the cleaver). The hue and cry caught up with him not much further down the street, searched him – nothing! Seems they'd got the wrong boy. (The cleaver rested for a moment,

47

balancing upright on the workbench.) Hue and cry? he says. What hue and cry? He was just running as fast as he could to fetch the doctor to his poor sick granny.

'Granny Smith!' muttered Jack.

'Aye!' said the butcher. 'That's right. That was the name. Do you know her? He must have thought that chicken was all right. He was back soon after, asking to buy it. Said a bowlful of chicken broth would be just the thing to set the old lady right.'

'But by then you'd sold it?' suggested Dr Watson.

'Taken it out the back to put the stuffing in, ready for Mrs H to collect. I offered him another, but he'd set his heart on that one. Very cut up about it, he was.'

'I bet he was,' muttered Jack, as soon as they were out of sight and sound of the butcher and his cleaver. 'He was the thief! That's where he hid the loot when they were after him.'

The doctor sighed. 'I must say I'm disappointed in Mrs Hudson. I always thought... She let me go on thinking that she made that stuffing herself. An old family

48

recipe. Ah, well!'

Fadge patted him sympathetically on the elbow. (It would have been the shoulder, if he could have reached it.) 'Life, eh?'

'As you say, Fadge. Such is life!' The doctor took out the locket and peered at it again in the dim light. 'It seems all we have to do now is find the lady! Why would a woman wearing a valuable locket be wandering on foot in this part of London?' he pondered. 'Unless –'

Fadge tugged at his sleeve, 'Put it away!' Glancing round, every shadow, every stray patch of mist, seemed to hold a promise of Rusty lurking in it. 'Let's get moving,' he said. And without waiting to see if they followed, he set off the way the cleaver had pointed.

'Good thinking!' murmured the doctor. 'Return to the scene of the crime, eh? See what that tells us!'

At the top of the road, they found nothing but a T-junction, with another narrow, dark street running across.

Behind them came a sudden yowl that might have been fighting alleycats, if you didn't know Rusty. It sent a shiver down Fadge's spine.

49

'Which way now?' pondered the doctor.

'This way!' Fadge said firmly, taking him by the arm, and heading for the bright lights and the people. The Masher wouldn't try anything while there were plenty of people around.

'Come on!' begged Fadge, pulling at the doctor's coat. 'We can lose 'em now!'

Jack, catching something of Fadge's panic, took a grip on the doctor's coat-tails and stuck close behind them.

9

Tasting the Reward

Seconds later, they were standing on a busy street, with horse-drawn cabs trotting by and chestnut sellers and ham-sandwich sellers and hot-potato men. The air was full of the smells of cooking, soot, stale fish, dog dirt and horse dung. The buildings were caked with grime and soot, the paint and plaster peeling off almost as fast as it was slapped on. Mud and slush were swept into swirling patterns by the ladies' skirts.

A tiny girl sang the first verse of 'The Last Rose of Summer', over and over. Nobody listened. Nobody gave her a farthing. So she launched into a wobbly tap-dance, to the tune of 'Rule Britannia', whistled by a blind man with a wooden leg and a sign saying 'Old Sojer. Pleas help' hung round his neck.

The blind man gave her a sour look when the first coin chinked into her begging bowl, not his; but he kept whistling. And she kept dancing.

A man in a top hat threw away the dog-end of a cigar, into the road. And a little kid was on it before it hit the ground, rescuing it from under the horses' flailing hooves.

Jack winced and watched till the kid made it safely back to the pavement.

No one else seemed especially bothered. Not even kind Dr Watson. He was gazing up at the building opposite with a rapt expression on his face.

Above the entrance 'Prince George Theatre' was painted in gold letters. Beside it stood a sandwich board, with a poster stuck to it:

TONIGHT at 7.00 pm
The Tragedy of HAMLET,
Prince of Denmark.
Mr BAILEY
to appear as
The Ghost of Hamlet's Father.

'I wonder!' the doctor muttered to himself.

'How does it go? Look thou upon this picture…
Could that be the answer? No sense standing
here wondering!' He launched himself across
the road without looking to the left or right.
And made it safely to the other side, where he
vanished between the theatre's white-painted
columns.

Fadge and Jack followed more cautiously,
dodging between the traffic. Which was why
they fetched up a little way down the street
and Jack's eye was caught by the other poster,
the one pasted onto the back of the sandwich
board:

LOST!!!
One GOLDEN PENDANT (and chain),
set with red and green stones.
In order to receive his JUST REWARD
the FINDER must apply (With All Speed!)
to Wm Bailey Esq, Actor-Manager,
at the Prince George Theatre.

'Reward!' breathed Fadge, after Jack had read
it out loud for him – twice, in case he'd heard
it wrong the first time. 'Where does it say
Reward?'

Jack pointed.

'That says re-ward? Come on, then!' Fadge grabbed Jack by the sleeve. 'Let's go and collect it!'

Off he went, up the steps, dragging Jack after him willy-nilly, through a foyer awash with red plush and gold leaf. To the first person he bumped into, 'Mr Bailey!' cried Fadge. 'Where is he? Where can I find him?'

Maybe it was his air of life-or-death urgency. Maybe the broom had something to do with it. A very large broom, bristles uppermost, jabbing at their chins. People gibbered and pointed and stood back out of Fadge's way, while the tall boy following close behind muttered, ''Scuse us! Cheers! Sorry!'

'What about Dr Watson?' Jack managed to get through to Fadge at last.

'He can catch up later.'

'But he's got the – Oh! No, he hasn't.'

Fadge twirled the pendant merrily round his head, then slipped it back inside his shirt.

'But I thought – When did you –?'

'Had to take it off him, didn't I? For his own safety. He don't know the Masher like I do.'

Jack hadn't got time to puzzle out how much safer Fadge thought the doctor would be without the pendant than with it, if the Masher thought he'd got it. Red plush and gold leaf had suddenly given way to bare boards and peeling plaster and a narrow winding staircase, leading upwards, with no hand-rail. Then a corridor, with plain wooden doors either side and names chalked on them.

'Which one's Bailey, then?' demanded Fadge. 'You can read, can't you?'

'Give me a chance. Some of them are smudged. This one looks like Mrs Bailey. We must be getting close. This is it! Wm Bailey, Esq, Actor and Manager,' Jack read aloud.

Fadge barged straight in without knocking.

10

Under Arrest

Following close behind, Jack saw walls flyposted with theatre bills from floor to ceiling, a smouldering fire in an open grate, and a screen in one corner gaudily hung with clothes. A thin-lipped young man in a tight suit glanced up as they erupted into the room. He was clutching a sheaf of papers, standing beside a desk, where an older man sat, totting up figures.

The older man did not look up. Jack felt he was making a point of not looking up.

'You Mr Bailey?' demanded Fadge.

'Sixty-two, sixty-four, sixty-five. That's three pounds, five shillings and fourpence for the gallery, Mr Musgrove,' the man at the table said to the thin young man, as if there was no one else in the room. 'Not bad, for a

Saturday night. Don't you agree?'

'It's good, Mr Bailey. Very good indeed.' The young man gave an uneasy glance towards Fadge. 'Er.'

The man at the table looked up.

Fadge gasped and drew back. The man's face was a mask of white, tinged with a graveyard green, the frown-lines etched dark and deep in his forehead and round his eyes. 'Yes?' His mouth leered blood-red.

Fadge got ready to run.

'It's just make-up,' hissed Jack, grabbing him. 'For the play. Remember the notice outside? Mr Bailey as the Ghost of Hamlet's father, right?' Then, still keeping tight hold of Fadge, 'Are you Wm Bailey Esq?'

'William Bailey Esquire?' boomed the actor-manager. 'I am! And who,' he paused, 'are you?'

'I'm Jack Farthing. And this is Fadge,' said Jack, dragging him forward.

'We found this,' said Fadge, pulling out the pendant. 'And we've come for the reward, like it said.'

'Have you, indeed!' Mr Bailey held out his hand.

Fadge drew back out of reach. 'What about the reward?'

'You shall have it!' The actor-manager picked up a little bell and rang it. 'Your just reward!'

Before Jack had quite made up his mind that he didn't much like the way Mr Bailey said that, the costume-draped screen gave a wobble. And a large man – a very large man! – in navy blue sidled out from behind it.

'What's this?' said Fadge.

'Constable!' commanded Mr Bailey. 'Do your duty!'

The policeman advanced.

Fadge stood firm. He dropped the pendant back inside his shirt, gripped his broom in both hands, and prepared to sell his freedom dearly.

'I never stole it!' yelled Fadge. 'And you're no policeman!'

'I arrest you –,' began the man in navy blue.

'Oh, no, you don't!' declared Fadge. 'Your buttons are wrong, for a start.'

The policeman – if policeman he was – still walking forward, looked down at his buttons to check, and met the end of the broom handle

58

coming the other way.

Young Mr Musgrove, caught up in the excitement, started towards Fadge, who dodged and fetched him a crack of the bristle end across the back of his knees that brought him down with a painful bump.

'Run for it, Jack!' cried Fadge. 'I'll hold 'em off! I never stole it!' he screeched at Mr Bailey. 'I found it! Like I said! I was bringing it back, like a good citizen! And this is all the thanks I get!' The broom was twirling like a windmill.

'Fadge!' yelled Jack.

'Haven't you gone yet?'

'I'm not going anywhere. Dr Watson! He's downstairs. He'll tell them. He'll tell them we found it. Found it inside the chicken. And we worked out how it got there. Listen to me, Fadge! Just listen!'

All four of them were suddenly listening, caught in a game of 'Statues'.

Jack said, 'Just put the broom down, Fadge, nice and slowly. Before you break it. You don't want to break it, do you, Fadge?'

Fadge bit his lip. 'I did find it. I did! And I want my reward.' It wasn't going to happen, was it? He knew it in his bones. Just like

59

he'd told the doctor: Life, eh! Life had a way of catching you a side-swipe, just when you thought you'd got it licked. But he put down the broom.

'Now!' Mr Bailey, safe behind his desk during all the excitement, took charge: 'Sam!' he said to the 'policeman', who was still nursing his bruised stomach, 'go downstairs, will you, and see if you can find this Dr Watson. Ask him to join us?' The navy-blue man grimaced, and left.

Mr Bailey pulled out a watch from under his ghostly robes. 'Act three, scene one. Queen Gertrude should have ten minutes to spare. Then there's the interval.' He gestured towards the door. 'Mr Musgrove!'

The thin young man went scurrying from the room.

11

Meeting the Queen

Mr Bailey, Jack and Fadge stood, or sat, eyeing each other. No one could think of anything to say. So they said nothing. Until the door was flung open. Queen Gertrude didn't walk into the room; she entered.

Every inch a queen, she looked, to Fadge's eyes anyway. Lips red as cherries, skin white as snow. Hair like a solid-gold crown, threaded with pearls. Dressed all in velvet and gold trimmings and lace coming out of her ears, almost.

'My dear!' Mr Bailey bowed low. 'My Queen!' (Mrs Bailey always liked to keep in character during a performance, or there was hell to pay after.) 'Good news!'

'Good news?' The Queen echoed, striking a pose, one hand behind her ear, the other on her heart.

'This child! This child of the gutter...'
Mr Bailey, overcome with emotion, flapped a
hand towards Fadge.

Fadge couldn't stand the suspense any
longer. He dragged out the locket again and
dangled it in front of her.

Queen Gertrude threw up her hands in
a pantomime of surprise and delight. 'It is
found!'

'Found!' Mr Bailey echoed. 'And is this
the boy?'

Queen Gertrude peered short-sightedly.
'Which boy? I can see two of them.'

'Either of them! Is either of these two boys
... the thief?' demanded Mr Bailey.

Faced with Mr Bailey's accusing finger,
the Masher would have fallen on his knees,
confessed and begged for mercy on the spot.

Queen Gertrude peered from Jack to
Fadge. 'No! A great lummox, I said, in a red
velvet coat.'

'He might have changed his coat.'

The Queen pressed one hand to her heart.
'I still say no! I'll take my oath on it!'

'Then how –?' Mr Bailey looked from

Fadge to Jack, who both stood lost for words.

Luckily at that moment, Dr Watson arrived, escorted by Sam in his navy blue, who took one look at Fadge still within arm's reach of his broom and beat a hasty retreat.

And Dr Watson told the story, from the beginning. 'Earlier this evening,' he began, 'this boy' – pointing at Jack – 'came knocking at my door...' The Baileys didn't just listen. They reacted. They had a pose for everything: mild interest, alarm, astonishment. An errand of mercy! A life-or-death race through dark, fog-bound streets! 'Meanwhile, back at the house...' said the doctor. And the Baileys turned to one another and nodded as if to say they'd suspected it all along.

Did they ever stop acting? Jack wondered. Did they wake up in the morning with loud yawns and stretchings and looking wide-eyed at one another, as if they'd never seen daylight before?

When they came to the crime and the hue and cry that followed, Queen Gertrude relived the moment. 'Gone! Gone for ever!' She whipped out a lace-trimmed handkerchief, and started dabbing at her blue-painted eyelids. 'My fault! I never should have worn it in the street!' she sobbed. 'Vanity! All is...'

'Vanity, thy name is woman!' Mr Bailey interrupted.

'Frailty, thy name is woman,' the Queen corrected, looking daggers.

'There, there!' cooed Mr Bailey. 'There's no harm done. It is found again!'

'Found.' She gave a brave, watery smile.

12

Fadge Finds His Role

There was a knock at the door. Mr Musgrove stuck his head round, 'Two minutes to the second half?'

'Give us five,' said Mr Bailey. 'Send on the clowns to fill in.' The door closed again. 'Dry your pretty eyes, my love. The locket is found, just in time for your big scene.' He whisked the necklace out of Fadge's fingers and slipped it over her head. 'Look thou upon this picture ... and on this?'

Fadge tugged at Dr Watson's sleeve. 'What's he talking about?'

'It's a line from the play,' whispered Dr Watson.

'Hamlet, Prince of Denmark?' said Jack.

'The greatest play ever written!' beamed Mr Bailey. 'This – that's the second "this", of course – being the locket that Hamlet wears, with the picture of his dead father, the Queen's first husband –'

'So noble, so brave, and so handsome!' The Queen was dabbing at her eyes again.

'That's me,' beamed Mr Bailey.

'Dead!' sighed the Queen. 'And my second husband, whose portrait I now wear ... that's this one here...'

'A villain!' growled Mr Bailey.

'His murderer!' The queen mimed shock-horror.

Fadge's head was starting to spin. He didn't want explanations. He wanted his reward.

'But if there ain't two lockets identical, where's the dramatic effect?' Mr Bailey spread his hands wide. 'I ask you!'

'So this locket,' said Jack. 'It's just a stage prop?'

Dr Watson shook his head. 'I thought as much. It was obvious that the picture inside was only meant to be seen from a distance. And when I couldn't find a goldsmith's mark, I realised the locket must be either very old, or –'

'Tat,' Fadge finished the sentence for him.

'So it's not worth anything? There's no reward?'

Mr Bailey looked uncomfortable. 'I was setting a trap for the thief. The thought of some honest citizen returning it was far from my thoughts. But what do you say to free tickets for the performance of your choice? Best seats in the house?'

Dr Watson nodded. 'I think that's a very fair offer. What about you, Fadge? And afterwards I'll treat you to the finest supper you've ever tasted! How about it?'

'If you want.' Fadge sadly picked up his broom.

Behind him, he heard Queen Gertrude give a little cry, 'Bill! It's him! It's Jo! We've found our Jo. Tell me it's not Jo to the life!'

Mr Bailey caught his breath. 'You think so, Bella?' he murmured, forgetting in his excitement that she was still Queen of Denmark.

So did she. 'Look at the way he moves, Bill. It's Jo.' She whisked out her blue-stained hankie and dabbed at her eyes again. 'I knew it! I knew there was something about him. The first moment I set eyes on him.'

'Boy!' boomed the actor-manager. 'You,

boy! Fadge! Turn round. Let me look at you.'

Slowly, broom in hand, Fadge turned, heart pounding in his breast. Always running a close second to his dream of The Reward came the one about turning out to be the Lost Heir. A rich man's beloved child, stolen from his cradle. Or a prince, lost in a shipwreck when a baby and raised by soft-hearted pirates. Long-lost child to these two? All right. He wasn't fussy.

'Let me see you walk!' commanded Mr Bailey.

Fadge, broom in hand, shuffled up and down a bit, then stood waiting for further instructions, while the Baileys put their heads together.

'You're right, my dear!'

'I'm always right!'

'It's Jo!'

Mrs Bella Bailey beamed. 'Jo, the Crossing Sweeper!'

'In *Bleak House*!' added Mr Bailey, turning to Fadge. 'It's a key part!'

'A marvellous part!'

'Not a dry eye in the house! "Dead, your majesty! Dead, ladies and gentlemen!" I forget the next bit... "And dying every day among us!"'

'Hang on a minute!' Fadge said nervously. 'I'm not planning to die. Not yet!'

'They're talking about a play, Fadge, I think,' said Jack. 'They're offering you a part in a play.'

'It's indoor work,' said the Queen.

'And no heavy lifting,' added Mr Bailey.

'Jo, the Crossing Sweeper!' exclaimed Dr Watson. 'I've read the book. The part's tailor-made for you, Fadge!'

'You've even got your own broom,' Jack pointed out.

Out of the rubble of yet another dream eluding him, Fadge struggled to build himself a different future. 'Do I get paid?' he asked.

There came another knock at the door and Mr Musgrove stuck his head round again. 'They're getting restless,' he said. 'I've got Sam doing his strong man act, but we can't hold them much longer.'

'We'll leave you with Mr Musgrove,' said the actor-manager, 'to sort out the details. Jo, the Crossing Sweeper, Mr Musgrove. *Bleak House*. The part is cast.' He picked up a cardboard crown that had been hanging on the back of his chair and, twirling it merrily round his finger, swept out, arm-in-arm with Queen Gertrude.

13

Don't Dob in Your Mates

I must have died and gone to heaven, Fadge kept thinking, as Dr Watson read out the contract Mr Musgrove drew up for him. Three meals a day, a place to bed down under the stage, and a share of the profits, if any, as pocket money. Paradise! He made his cross on the dotted line.

'There is just one thing,' smirked Mr Musgrove, with his pen poised over the paper, a smudge and a blot away from making it all legal and Bristol-fashion. 'The name of the person – or persons – who did steal the locket?'

'Does it matter?' asked Jack.

Mr Musgrove had been pencilled in for Jo the Crossing Sweeper, though he was too tall by half, before Fadge happened along.

Mr Musgrove gave a smirk. 'Loyalty among thieves, is it? If the Law comes asking, Fadge, – and they will come, 'cause Mrs Bailey reported the locket missing. I'm sure they'll be delighted to hear she's got it back but, well, I'll have to tell them, won't I? About your part in this business and that you might be able to help them with their enquiries.'

'You'd better tell him, Fadge,' said Jack.

Fadge hung his head. 'Don't know their proper names,' he muttered. 'Nor where they live. I don't know nothing.'

'Come on, Fadge,' muttered the doctor. 'They're bad lots, both of them. Sooner or later the Law's bound to catch up with them.'

'Don't know nothing,' said Fadge again, so quietly, they barely heard. So help him, he couldn't do it. Not if his life depended on it.

He caught Jack's eye.

Jack understood. Don't dob in your mates. Even if they're not your mates.

'I've got an idea,' said Jack. He whispered in Fadge's ear. Fadge caught on quick. By the time Jack finished, Fadge was almost doing flip-flaps, like a fish let off the hook.

Jack said, 'We'll need to borrow the locket

72

for a while.'

'Why?' Mr Musgrove looked at him narrowly. If he made himself any narrower, he'd disappear down one of the cracks between the floorboards and good riddance.

'You don't need to know that,' said Jack. 'But I promise you'll get it back.'

'I'll leave my broom, if you like,' offered Fadge. 'As a hostage, sort of.'

Mr Musgrove laid down his pen. 'I'll ask,' he said. 'As soon as Mr Bailey comes off stage.'

14

The Music Returns

'But are you really sure,' the doctor asked, as they made their way back the way they'd come, 'that you can persuade these – friends – of yours to give themselves up?'

'Don't you worry about it,' mumbled Fadge, through a mouthful of gingerbread the doctor had bought for him at the last stall they passed. Jack said he wasn't hungry, so Fadge felt it was up to him to let the doctor be generous if he wanted to. But it was hard work, getting through it all on his own. The ham sandwich and the pocketful of peas and the toffee apple and the chestnuts.

'You really think they'll fall for it?' said Jack.

Fadge gave a loud burp – 'Pardon!' – before he answered. 'They're not too bright. Or they'd never have thought that was real gold and jewels in the first place.'

Jack didn't think this was the time to remind Fadge that he'd been fooled himself, the first time he saw the locket.

As they moved away from the lights and the traffic, he started wondering: how long had he been here, stuck in this time zone, whatever? Hours, it must be. How was he going to explain it away when he got back? *If* he got back. Somewhere he'd read about hundreds of people going missing every year. What if just a few somehow slipped down some kind of crack in time and never managed to claw their way out again? What if he ended up as one of them?

Mum and Grandad waiting and waiting for him to come back with the shopping. Grandad would be sick as a parrot if there was no All-Bran for his breakfast in the morning.

And then...

'Listen!' said Jack. 'I can hear a barrel organ.' Playing a half-familiar tune...

'Won't you buy my pretty flowers?' the doctor sang along, then went on pom-pomming when he ran out of words, beating time with his hand.

'Silly thing to be playing, this time of year,' mumbled Fadge, taking another swig of ginger beer from the bottle. 'No flowers around now.'

'Where's it coming from?' asked Jack. The barrel organ! That was when it all began. With the music of the barrel organ.

And the fog came tumbling out of the side alleys and up from the area steps where it had lain, biding its time, between then and now.

'Where's it coming from? The music?' Jack turned and turned. Listening, trying to get a fix. This way? That way! There! Where the fog was gathering, thickening to a marmalade-yellow, billowing upwards and outwards, smelling of rotten eggs and stale fish. This was his chance – maybe his only chance. 'I've got to go! There's Grandad's shopping to do and Mum'll be getting worried.' But if he went now – he glanced down at Fadge – he'd never know what happened. Could Fadge possibly deal with the Masher and Rusty on his own?

Fadge swallowed. 'You go on.'

'You'll be all right?'

'All the better for not having to look after you, Jack Farthing.'

'Yeah.' Jack forced a smile. 'Cheers, then.'

'What about the theatre?' called the doctor.

'The theatre?' asked Jack, hands in his pockets, walking backwards, still keeping his options open.

'Hamlet, Prince of Denmark. Best seats in the house?'

'I don't know. I'll try and make it. If I can't, you'd better take your friend instead.'

'My friend?'

'The one who's coming to help you eat that chicken, remember?'

'Oh, lord!' Doctor Watson clapped a hand to his head. 'The chicken! We left it on the kitchen table, stuffing half-in, half-out.'

'Take care, right?' said Jack.

Then he turned and walked away, into the fog, towards the jangling music.

'He's dropped his scarf!' Fadge darted forward, scooped it up and stood peering helplessly into the wall of fog. 'I'll look after it for him, shall I? Till he comes back.'

He draped the scarf round his neck. He'd fancied that scarf, the first time he set eyes on it. Blue and white stripes, with lettering.

The doctor was chuckling to himself. 'Stolen

goods hidden inside a chicken! I must tell my friend when he comes tomorrow. He collects odd stories. Sometimes he writes them down.'

'A writing-gentleman? Is he famous? What's his name?'

'He's not famous. His name's Doyle.' From somewhere beyond the swirling wall of fog, Jack caught the echo of the doctor's voice. 'Dr Arthur Conan Doyle.'

He wanted to turn round, go back, ask the doctor if he meant *the* Arthur Conan Doyle, the one who wrote *Sherlock Holmes*, even though the doctor said he'd never heard of Sherlock Holmes.

But there was no turning back now. He set off towards the familiar sound of traffic and the bright lights of the supermarket.

15

A Happy Trap

Fadge was on his own, slouching along with his hands in his pockets, in the opposite direction from the one the doctor had taken.

He'd had a bit of trouble shaking the doctor off. Persuading him he didn't need protection. Told him first he ought to go home to deal with that chicken. Told him second that the Masher would never come near if he saw the doctor lurking. Finished up by saying angrily, 'What's the matter? Don't you trust me with Mrs B's locket? That's it, isn't it? You don't trust me!'

So now he was on his own. No need to go looking for the Masher and Rusty. They'd find him soon enough. He wished he had his broom for company. He tried to whistle, but his mouth was dry, in spite of the bottle of ginger beer he'd just poured down his throat.

When the attack came, they took him completely by surprise, closing in from both sides at once, pinning him up against the wall.

'Oi! Gerroff!' said Fadge. The Masher backed off to arm's length, keeping his hand splayed against Fadge's chest, while Fadge dusted himself down.

'Where've you been?' demanded the Masher.

'Up the town,' Fadge said truthfully. He cut off more questions by counter-attacking. 'You ran off and left me. What did you go and do that for?'

The Masher took his hand away. Maybe he was just a bit ashamed, though Fadge wouldn't have bet ready money on it. 'No sense in all three of us getting caught.'

'It was that Jack's fault,' grumbled Rusty. 'Bringing the doctor back with him before we finished the job.'

'Where is he, anyway?' asked the Masher.

'Who? The doctor?'

'Your cousin.'

'My cousin Jack? He had to go home.'

'Good riddance!' rasped Rusty.

Fadge glowered at him.

'Anyway,' said the Masher. 'We thought, best leave you to talk your way out. You being so small and pathetic and all.'

Fadge forced a grin. 'Poor starving child tempted by a larder window that shouldn't have been left open in the first place?'

'Yeah!' The others grinned back.

Fadge stopped grinning. 'Poor starving child that had had his dinner stolen from under his nose! But I forgive you,' he said nobly. 'Because that doctor took pity on this poor, starving child. He took us up the town and he bought me a ham sandwich and a pocketful of peas, and gingerbread, and a toffee apple, and flapjack, and a bottle of ginger beer to wash it down. And hot chestnuts.' He rummaged in his pockets. 'I still got some left.' He took out a grubby paper bag. 'You want one?'

They shook their heads.

'P'raps you'd rather have this?' He pulled out his other hand. There was something in it. Something shining golden in the gaslight, with a twinkling of red and green stones.

It was so unexpected, at first Rusty and the Masher just stood and gazed at Queen Gertrude's locket, swinging gently before their eyes – to and fro, to and fro – like two boys hypnotised.

Then, 'Gimme!' cried the Masher, snatching at it and missing by a mile.

Fadge danced away.

'That's what you were after. Wasn't it, Masher? Wasn't it, Rusty?' The look on their faces! Fadge tossed the prize from hand to hand and back again. 'Wasn't no chicken you wanted, it was what was inside it! Hey, Masher? Hey, Rusty?' Every time the Masher reached out to grab it, the locket was somewhere else. 'Soon as I twigged, I came looking for you two, so we could all claim the reward together.'

'Reward?' demanded the Masher, suddenly pulled up short.

'Reward?' wheezed Rusty, a dying echo.

'Better than trying to sell it, eh?' Fadge rattled on. 'The Police must be onto it by now, if there's a reward offered.'

'What reward?'

'There's a poster up outside the theatre,' he told them. 'LOST, it said, one golden pendant set with red and green stones. Then something about a reward.'

'Wait a minute! You can't read.' said Rusty.

'I've got ears. I heard someone read it out,' Fadge said patiently. 'Lost, it said. And a reward offered. Only if I'd taken it in and told them I found it inside a chicken, they would never have believed me. Where did you find it, Masher?'

'Find it?' Rusty was still getting his head round the idea of giving the pendant back to the person it belonged to. 'Wait a minute, Masher. She knows you, don't she? Saw you when you snatched...'

'Shut up, Rusty! I'm thinking. She saw me stopped and searched and I was clean as a whistle. And I was sorry for the lady – wasn't I? – losing a valuable locket like that. So we hung around and looked, didn't we? And we found it, where the thief threw it away, because they were after him. But we're not telling you, Fadge, where we found it. So you'd better just give us it and we'll split the reward three ways, like you said. That's fair, isn't it?'

'Fair enough,' said Fadge, hanging on tight to the locket, ready to skip out of reach. Make a run for it if he had to.

'Hand it over, then.'

'Which theatre was it?'

'Don't know the name of it,' said Fadge. 'Can't read, can I, Rusty? But I can show you. I'll hold onto the goods till we get there, shall I, Masher? I'd like to have it just a little bit longer. Please, Masher?'

Just in case they changed their minds on the way and decided to skip with it after all.

Luckily the Masher was feeling generous. He let Fadge keep the locket all the way back to the theatre.

The Masher peered at the billboard, struggling to make sense of it. 'L-o-s-t.' That was a good start. He stood back. 'You read it, Rusty. Read it out loud, so Fadge can hear.'

Painfully slowly Rusty spelled out the words, one speckled finger following the letters along. 'Lost! Yes. One gol-den...' Years of Fadge's life seemed to pass, it took so long. Some of the words Rusty had to make up, so 'receive' came out as 'get' and 'apply' turned into 'ask' – but he was close enough.

'Ba-iley! Right!' said the Masher. 'Give me that! You wait here, Fadge.'

Meekly, Fadge handed over the prize.

They'd earned it. 'Whatever you say, Masher.'

He crossed to the other side of the street, so as to have a good view. Then he waited, like the Masher had told him to do, while the two of them walked into Mr Bailey's trap.

'Beautiful!' murmured Fadge, when they came out again. A sight for sore eyes: Rusty and the Masher collared by a policeman, one in each beefy hand, and both hollering fit to bust that it was a stitch-up! A fit-up! They'd been framed!

'No sense in all three of us getting caught, eh, Masher?' he grinned to himself. Then he gave a deep sigh, mainly of happiness, partly of indigestion, and made his way round to the stage door, where his broom and his new life were waiting.

Watching from the window of a nearby tavern, young Dr Watson lifted his pint pot and drank a toast to Fadge and his rather odd friend.

16

The Slips Revealed

'What happened to your scarf?' said Mum to Jack, as she took the shopping from him. And that was all she said. Nothing about 'Where have you been gone to all this time?' and 'I've been worried sick!' like when he went round to Gary's to deliver a geography textbook they'd been sharing and stayed to watch the football.

'My scarf?'

'Your Millwall scarf I knitted you. Weren't you wearing it when you went out?'

'Oh, that! Was I?'

He sure as heck wasn't going out again to look for it! He was back where he belonged, and planning to stay. Still wondering what happened to Fadge, though.

In the front room, Grandad was still

watching *Sherlock Holmes*.

Jack stood in the doorway for a bit. 'I remember this one,' he said slowly. '*The Case of the Blue Carbuncle*, right? The blue carbuncle. It's a stolen jewel. It's hidden inside the chicken, isn't it?'

'The goose,' said Grandad, without turning round.

'Whatever. The thief hid it inside the goose.'

'The goose swallowed it.'

'Oh, right. Grandad?'

'What?' Grandad punched the pause button. 'You got something to say, then say it.'

'Sherlock Holmes. You said there was no such person.'

'That's right.'

'What about Dr Watson, though? I mean, it's quite an ordinary sort of name. What if there really was a Dr Watson?'

'Bound to have been. Lots of them.'

'That's what I thought. And who wrote the stories?'

'Arthur Conan Doyle.'

'Dr Arthur Conan Doyle?'

'Yes! He was a doctor. Started off with a practice in – where was it?'

'Southsea?'

'That's right. Why all these questions?'

'Just making sure I remembered it right.'

As Jack climbed the stairs to the attic, he heard the programme getting underway again. Dr Watson's voice sounding gruff and kind of elderly, not very bright. Nothing like the Dr Watson he'd met.

He sank down onto a moth-eaten tapestry foot stool, beside an old tin trunk painted an unlovely shade of green. For want of anything better to do, he flipped open the lid of the trunk. Inside were stacks of yellowing paper. Old account books. Letters tied up in bundles. Postcards and brown photographs. Theatre programmes. Pages of old newspapers. As he rifled through, a single photo fluttered out from among the rest and lay upside-down on the floor at his feet, waiting for him to pick it up.

The back was printed like a postcard. No writing. No stamp. Jack turned it over. There was a picture on the front. A picture of a boy about his own age. Underneath, it said: Master Jack Farthing, as 'Jo, the Crossing

Sweeper' in *Bleak House*. Looking sternly up at him was Fadge.

Jack grabbed the photo and went tumbling down the stairs again. 'Grandad! Grandad!'

Grandad sighed and pressed the pause button again, 'What is it now?'

'Grandad, were you ever on the stage?'

'No.'

Jack thrust the photo under his nose, 'Is this you?'

The old man shook his head, disgusted. 'I'm not that old. That's my grandad.'

'You never told me about him.'

'It was a long time ago. Anyway, you never asked.'

'I'm asking now. Everything you can remember.'

'That's not much.' Grandad took the photo. 'He was just a little feller. Smaller than you when he was full-grown, so he never got to play the hero, just what they call character parts.' He thought for a bit, chewing on nothing. 'I saw him in a play once.' Another pause for thought. 'He made me laugh and he made me cry, I remember that. Oh, yes! What was that play called?'

Jack said, 'There's a load of programmes and stuff upstairs. Shall I bring them down?'

'Yes,' said Grandad, still half lost in memories. 'You do that.'

From the kitchen, Mum heard a rumbling like thunder down the stairs, but nobody yelled, so she didn't go out. After that, a long silence. No telly. That was worrying.

When she eased open the front-room door, she saw Grandad still in his chair, with Jack sitting on the floor at his feet, the two of them marooned on a little island in a sea of paper.

Grandad was saying, 'Jack Farthing – that's my grandad – he had three children, Young Jack, Bella and George.'

George, thought Jack: after the Prince George Theatre, where he had his first acting job? Bella. After Mrs Bella Bailey?

Grandad went on, 'George was my dad. Young Jack – who would have been my uncle – he was killed in the First World War. A place they called Wipers. He was just turned twenty.'

Poor Fadge. After all the knocks he'd taken. Picked himself up, dusted himself down.

Life, eh? He was going to lose his eldest son. 'Poor Fadge!'

'Fadge, yes. That's what they called him. I don't know why. Something to do with him being so small.'

'A fadge was a farthing.'

'Was it? I didn't know that.'

'That's a small brown coin…'

'I know what a farthing is! Kept all Young Jack's badges he did. And the Bible he gave him.' Grandad was chewing again, on nothing. 'There was a great trade in Bibles in those days. Small enough to fit in a breast pocket, just over your heart. Thick enough to stop a bullet. They must be in here somewhere.' He was rummaging through the stuff at the bottom of the trunk.

'There's three or four trunks more up in the attic,' said Jack, starting towards the door. Was it possible he'd met his own great-great-grandad? He wanted proof; proof that he hadn't just dreamed it all. Made it up out of names and scraps and maybe – yes – even a photograph seen once and then forgotten.

He caught a brief glimpse of Mum's back, retreating to the kitchen again, which was maybe just as well, because she didn't see what happened next. Behind him he heard Grandad still muttering to himself, 'They've got to be here somewhere. Huh? What's this?'

Turning, he saw the old man, like a conjuror producing the flags of all nations, pulling something from under the debris at the bottom of the trunk. A knitted scarf. The stripes had faded to greyish-white and bluey-grey, during a hundred years or more. But Jack recognised it, from where Mum had counted the stitches wrong and turned the final 'L' to an 'I'.

'His lucky scarf!' said Grandad. 'That's what he always called it. Odd, though, because he was never a Millwall supporter. He told me once it was something to do with his first acting job.' He sighed and shook his head. 'I suppose it's just one of those things we'll never know.'

Glossary

Barrel organ   A small instrument, played by turning a handle.

Cleaver   A tool for chopping meat.

Concertina   A small musical instrument.

Dripping   Melted fat from roasting meat.

Eiderdown   A quilt filled with down.

Farthing   A coin; a quarter of a penny.

Guinea   A coin; one pound.

Home Guard   The British Citizen Army, organised to defend the UK against invasion. Founded in 1940.

Lummox   A clumsy, stupid person.

Sheltered Housing   Semi-independent accommodation for the elderly, with some shared facilities and a warden.

Shilling   A coin; twelve pence.

Siren song   The call of something appealing but potentially dangerous.

Snakesman   A boy skilled at entering houses through small spaces, for criminal purposes.

Wipers (Ypres)   The location of many battles during the First World War.

Historical Note

At any time during Queen Victoria's reign there were around 30,000 children sleeping rough in London. That's not counting those fending for themselves who had somewhere to go at night – which might be just a few square metres of someone else's one-room flat, screened off by a blanket. Some of them cared for younger brothers and sisters, too.

If they didn't work, they starved. So they sold things like flowers, flypapers, peg-dolls, cigars, matches or bundles of firewood; they sang songs or they danced; they scavenged in the gutters and among the rubbish for anything they could sell on for a penny or two: rags, bones, cigar ends, even dog turds (which were used to soften the leather for making gloves).

The alternative was the workhouse, where conditions were made deliberately harsh, to put off scroungers. Even prison was more comfortable, according to one boy who was sent to jail for a month for begging.

The nicest place he'd ever been, he said; next time he'd make sure he was put inside for theft, so they'd keep him a bit longer.

The London fogs known as pea-soupers happened all through the 19th century and up until the middle of the 20th. By this time they were worse, because the exhaust fumes from cars and buses were added to the brew. The smog in the winter of 1952 caused the deaths of over 4,000 people. In 1956, the Government passed the Clean Air Act, which banned the use of coal fires in London and cut down industrial pollution.

There was no such person as Sherlock Holmes. Sir Arthur Conan Doyle based him and his method of deduction on careful observation of a professor who taught him at medical school in Edinburgh, Dr Joseph Bell. Ever since the stories first appeared, people have written to the great detective at 221B, Baker Street, asking for his help.

Other books in the series:

Final Victory • Herbie Brennan

Across the Roman Wall • Theresa Breslin

A Candle in the Dark • Adèle Geras

Soldier's Son • Garry Kilworth

Casting the Gods Adrift • Geraldine McCaughrean

Out of the Shadow • Margaret Nash

Blitz Boys • Linda Newbery

Doodlebug Summer • Alison Prince

A Ghost-light in the Attic • Pat Thomson

Voyage of the Silver Bream • Theresa Tomlinson

Mission to Marathon • Geoffrey Trease

Gunner's Boy • Ann Turnbull